Green Light Readers
For the new reader who's ready to GO!

Amazing adventures await every young child who is eager to read.

Green Light Readers encourage children to explore, to imagine, and to grow through books. Created for beginning readers at two levels of skill, these lively illustrated stories have been carefully developed to reinforce reading basics taught at school and to make reading a fun and rewarding experience for children and grown-ups to share outside the classroom.

The grades and ages within each skill level are general guidelines only, and books included in both levels may feature any or all of the bulleted characteristics. When choosing a book for a new reader, remember that every child progresses at his or her own pace—be patient and supportive as the magic of reading takes hold.

1 Buckle up!
Kindergarten–Grade 1: Developing reading skills, ages 5–7
  • Short, simple stories • Fully illustrated • Familiar objects and situations
  • Playful rhythms • Spoken language patterns of children
  • Rhymes and repeated phrases • Strong link between text and art

2 Start the engine!
Grades 1–2: Reading with help, ages 6–8
  • Longer stories, including nonfiction • Short chapters
  • Generously illustrated • Less-familiar situations
  • More fully developed characters • Creative language, including dialogue
  • More subtle link between text and art

Green Light Readers incorporate characteristics detailed in the Reading Recovery model used by educators to assess the readability of texts through the end of first grade. Guidelines for reading levels for these readers have been developed with assistance from Mary Lou Meerson. An educational consultant, Ms. Meerson has been a classroom teacher, a language arts coordinator, an elementary school principal, and a university professor.

Published in collaboration with Harcourt Brace School Publishers

Catch Me
If You Can!

Bernard Most

Green Light Readers
Harcourt Brace & Company
San Diego   New York   London

Printed in Hong Kong

He was the biggest dinosaur of them all.
The other dinosaurs were afraid of him.

When the biggest dinosaur went by,
the other dinosaurs quickly hid.

They were afraid of his great big tail.

They were afraid of his great big claws.

They were afraid of his great big feet.

But most of all, they were afraid of his great big teeth.

One little dinosaur wasn't afraid.
She didn't run. She didn't hide.

"Catch me if you can!" she called
to the biggest dinosaur.

"I'm not afraid of your great big tail.

Catch me if you can!"

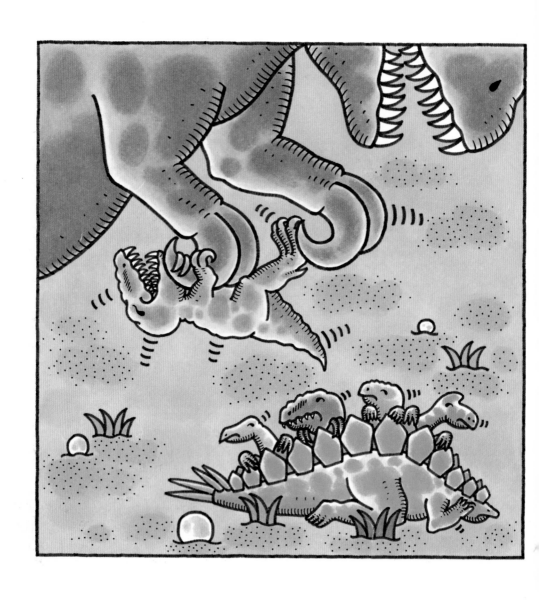

"I'm not afraid of your great big claws.

Catch me if you can!"

"I'm not afraid of your great big feet.

Catch me if you can!"

"And most of all, I'm not afraid of your great big teeth."

"I can catch you!" said the biggest dinosaur.
And he grabbed the little dinosaur.

But she only got a big hug.
"I love you very much, Grandpa!"
said the little dinosaur.

"And I love you, too!"
said the biggest dinosaur of them all.

Requests for permission to make copies of any part of the work should be mailed to:
Permissions Department, Harcourt Brace & Company, 6277 Sea Harbor Drive,
Orlando, Florida 32887-6777.

First Green Light Readers edition 1999
Green Light Readers is a trademark of Harcourt Brace & Company.

The Library of Congress has cataloged the original paperback edition as follows:
Most, Bernard.
Catch me if you can!/Bernard Most.
p. cm.
"Green Light Readers."
Summary: When a little dinosaur plays a game with the biggest dinosaur
of them all, she's not scared because he's her grandpa.
[1. Dinosaurs—Fiction. 2. Grandfathers—Fiction.] I. Title.
PZ7.M8544Cat 1999
[E]—dc21   98-15569
ISBN 0-15-202001-2 (pb)

ISBN 0-15-202351-8

B D F G E C (pb)

A C E F D B

Meet the Author-Illustrator

**Bernard Most knew he wanted to be an
artist even before he went to kindergarten.
Later, he went to art school and became
an artist. He saw some books by Leo Lionni
and liked them so much that he started to
write his own books for children.**

**Bernard Most works hard on his books.
He sent out one book forty-two times
before it was published! He didn't give up.
He knows how important it is to believe
in yourself and to keep trying.**

Walt Chrynwski

Bernard Most

Look for these other Green Light Readers—
all affordably priced in paperback!

Level 1/Kindergarten–Grade 1

Big Brown Bear
David McPhail

Cloudy Day/Sunny Day
Donald Crews

Down on the Farm
Rita Lascaro

Popcorn
Alex Moran
Illustrated by Betsy Everitt

Sometimes
Keith Baker

What I See
Holly Keller

Level 2/Grades 1–2

A Bed Full of Cats
Holly Keller

The Chick That Wouldn't Hatch
Claire Daniel
Illustrated by Lisa Campbell Ernst

The Fox and the Stork
Gerald McDermott

I Wonder
Tana Hoban

Shoe Town
Janet Stevens and Susan Stevens Crummel
Illustrated by Janet Stevens

The Very Boastful Kangaroo
Bernard Most

Green Light Readers is a trademark of Harcourt Brace & Company.

Green Light Readers
For the new reader who's ready to GO!